English Extra

Extra

Activity Book

GRACE TANAKA AND KAY FERRELL

Longman

Publisher: Mary Jane Peluso
Development Editor: Margaret Grant
Director of Production and Manufacturing: Aliza Greenblatt
Executive Managing Editor: Dominick Mosco
Electronic Production Editor: Carey Davies
Manufacturing Manager: Ray Keating

Electronic Art Production Supervisor: Ken Liao
Electronic Art Production Specialist: Steven Greydanus
Cover Design: Carey Davies
Art Director: Merle Krumper
Interior Design: Carey Davies

Illustrator: Betsy Day

10   9   8   7   6

ISBN   0-13-872029-0

UNIT	Title	Pages
1	How are you?	1–8
2	What do you do on Saturdays?	9–16
3	Can we buy some ice cream?	17–24
4	Can you identify items in this kitchen?	25–32
5	I like shopping at Dutton's Department Store.	33–40
6	Where do you want to go?	41–48
7	What's the emergency?	49–56
8	Health Information Form.	57–64
9	Watch out for the cars!	65–72
10	Job board.	73–80
11	What's in the office?	81–88
12	Do you want to live here?	89–96
13	It's a deal!	97–104
14	Bic, you're lazy at home.	105–112
15	Celebration!	113–120

English Extra

GRACE TANAKA AND KAY FERRELL

Activity Workbook

How are you?

A. Read the words.

1. angry
2. great
3. so–so

4. bored
5. happy
6. tired

7. fine
8. sad
9. upset

10. good
11. sick

B. Write the word under the picture.

a. She is _h a p p y_.

b. She is _s _ _ _.

c. He is _u _ _ _ _ _.

d. She is _f _ _ _ _.

e. She is _g _ _ _ _.

f. He is _s _ _ – _ _.

g. She is _a _ _ _ _ _.

h. He is _t _ _ _ _ _.

i. She is _b _ _ _ _.

j. He is _s _ _ _.

k. She is _g _ _ _ _ _.

Do you know the alphabet letters?

A. Read and write the alphabet letters.

A _A_ a _a_,   B ___ b ___,   C ___ c ___,

D ___ d ___,   E ___ e ___,   F ___ f ___,

G ___ g ___,   H ___ h ___,   I ___ i ___,

J ___ j ___,   K ___ k ___,   L ___ l ___,

M ___ m ___,   N ___ n ___,   O ___ o ___,

P ___ p ___,   Q ___ q ___,   R ___ r ___,

S ___ s ___,   T ___ t ___,   U ___ u ___,

V ___ v ___,   W ___ w ___,   X ___ x ___,

Y ___ y ___,   Z ___ z ___

B. Write the missing letters.

a	b		d		f	
h			k	l		
o		q	r		t	
v		x				

Do you remember the numbers?

A. Read and write the numbers.

1	2			5			8		10
11		13			16			19	20
	22		24				28		
		33				37			
	42			46					
51		53							
				66					
		73							
			85					89	90
	92				96			99	100

B. Write the number words.

1. one _____
2. two _____
3. three _____
4. four _____
5. five _____

6. six _____
7. seven _____
8. eight _____
9. nine _____
10. ten _____

11. eleven _____
12. twelve _____
13. thirteen _____
14. fourteen _____
15. fifteen _____

C. Read and write the missing numbers.

a.

6	8		12		16		

b.

18	20		24		28		32

c.

3	6		12		18		24

Our Classroom

1. board	5. clock	9. pencil sharpener
2. bookcase	6. computer	10. projector
3. calculator	7. flag	11. screen
4. calendar	8. map	12. wheelchair

B. Write the word under the picture.

a. _____computer_____

b. _____

c. _____

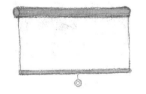

d. _____

e. _____

f. _____

g. _____

h. _____

i. _____

j. _____

k. _____

l. _____

Your Identification Card

1. 555-9865   a. first name
2. Spring Valley   b. zip code
3. Sue   c. address
4. 92234   d. telephone number
5. 142 Pine Street   e. last name
6. (619)   f. state
7. CA   g. Social Security Number
8. Apple   h. area code
9. 576-34-2345   i. city

 B. Complete the form. Write about you.

Duttonville School
Please Print

Date: _____
             month   *date*   *year*

Sex: M _____   **Marital Status:** Single   _____
         F _____   Married   _____
                                                         Divorced _____

Name: _____
               (last)   *(first)*

Address: _____
                 (number–street)   *(apt.)*

            _____ _____ _____
              (city)   *(state)*   *(zip code)*

Telephone: (   ) _____

Social Security number _____ – _____ – _____

Signature _____

My name is . . .

A. Read about Sue Apple.

My name is Sue Apple.

I am married.

I live in Spring Valley, California.

I am happy today.

B. Draw a picture of you.

C. Write about you.

My name is _____.

I am _____. (married/ single)

I live in _____, _____.
                city   *state*

I am _____ today.

(angry, bored, fine, good, great, happy, sad, sick, so-so, tired, upset)

D. Write your story here.

_____

_____

_____

_____

UNIT 1 Crossword Puzzle

¹B	O	A	R	D		

Across

1.

4.

6.

9.

10.

board
bookcase
calculator
calendar
clock
computer
flag
map
projector
screen
wheelchair

Down

1.

2.

3.

5.

7.

8.

UNIT 1 Wordsearch

```
N   T   Q   D   W   M   X   J   S   T   R   E   E   T   M   R
A   U   X   I   Z   N   B   M   C   N   V   C   P   Q   N   F
M   C   G   D   U   S   I   N   G   L   E   A   F   M   K   J
E   C   H   I   A   M   K   U   S   H   V   R   O   A   X   S
G   R   R   V   Y   V   O   H   W   R   I   T   E   R   N   C
E   A   E   O   V   E   W   O   T   C   P   X   Q   R   S   H
C   O   A   R   L   I   S   T   E   N   D   R   V   I   D   O
H   K   D   C   Z   O   W   S   X   Q   S   N   T   E   O   O
H   A   Z   E   F   K   B   M   S   T   A   T   E   D   O   L
D   D   K   D   F   C   I   T   Y   F   E   M   A   L   E   K
K   D   T   A   N   P   F   K   A   C   I   R   C   L   E   F
U   R   N   M   W   S   S   X   D   M   X   A   U   M   Q   M
P   E   Q   H   A   S   S   L   Z   B   C   O   W   A   N   P
P   S   T   E   L   E   P   H   O   N   E   W   N   L   O   I
Z   S   V   R   Q   B   P   Y   J   L   T   S   M   E   W   K
A   Q   E   V   T   J   C   T   F   M   P   I   Z   H   Z   A
```

___ ADDRESS   ___ CITY   ___ STATE   ✓ NAME

___ MALE   ___ FEMALE   ___ SINGLE   ___ DIVORCED

___ MARRIED   ___ TELEPHONE   ✓ STREET   ___ LISTEN

___ READ   ___ WRITE   ___ CIRCLE   ___ SCHOOL

What do you do on Saturdays?

Do you shop on Saturdays?   Yes, I do.   I shop on Saturdays.

No, I don't.   I don't shop on Saturdays.

Write about you.

1. Do you _____rest_____ on Saturdays?

____Yes, I do____.

____I rest on Saturdays____.

2. Do you _____ on Saturdays?

_____.

_____.

3. Do you _____ on Saturdays?

_____.

_____.

4. Do you _____ on Saturdays?

_____.

_____.

Do you know the days of the week?

A. Write the names of the days of the week.

Fill in the blanks.   Write the days.

1. S _u_ nd _a_ y   _Sunday_   _Sunday_

2. M ___ nd ___ y   _____   _____

3. T ___ esd ___ y   _____   _____

4. W ___ dne ___ d ___ y   _____   _____

5. Th ___ r ___ d ___ y   _____   _____

6. F ___ id ___ y   _____   _____

7. S ___ tu ___ d ___ y   _____   _____

B. Make a calendar for this month. Ask your teacher for help.

_____   _____
       month   year

S_____	_____	_____	_____	_____	_____	_____

C. Practice with your teacher: Today is _____.

Tomorrow is _____.

Yesterday was _____.

What time is it?

A. Match the times.

1. ___d___

a.

2. _____

b.

3. _____

c.

4. _____

d.

5. _____

e.

B. Draw the hour and minute hands on the clock face.

12:05	12:00	1:30	10:45
4:00	8:15	7:15	6:45

11
● ● ● ●

Can you identify the furniture?

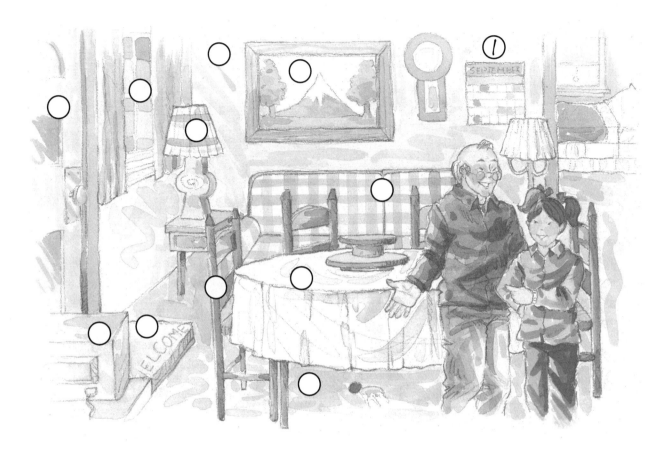

A. Identify each item in the picture above and write the number in the circle.

1. calendar	2. chair	3. door	4. floor
calendar	_____	_____	_____
5. lamp	6. picture	7. rug	8. sofa
_____	_____	_____	_____
9. table	10. television	11. wall	12. window
_____	_____	_____	_____

B. Read and write each word above.

What's in your living room?

A. Draw a picture of your living room.

B. Write a list of things you have in your living room.
Ask your teacher for help with new words.

_____ _____ _____

_____ _____ _____

_____ _____ _____

_____ _____ _____

_____ _____ _____

_____ _____ _____

Tell me about your family.

| How many | brothers
sisters
sons
daughters | do you have? | I have | one brother.
two sisters.
three sons.
four daughters. |

A. Ask your classmates. Write the answers.

Name	Brothers	Sisters	Sons	Daughters

B. Look at the chart. Complete the sentences.

1. _____ has the most brothers.
       (name)

   _____ has _____ brothers.
   (He/She)

2. _____ has the most sisters.
       (name)

   _____ has _____ sisters.
   (He/She)

3. _____ has the most sons.
       (name)

   _____ has _____ sons.
   (He/She)

4. _____ has the most daughters.
       (name)

   _____ has ____ daughters.
   (He/She)

UNIT 2 Crossword Puzzle

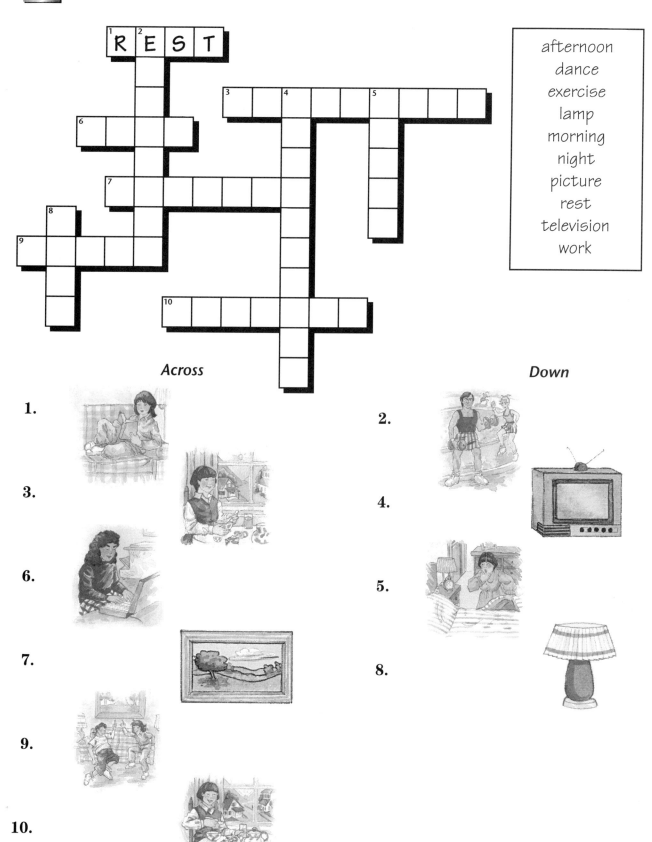

¹R ²E S T

afternoon
dance
exercise
lamp
morning
night
picture
rest
television
work

Across

1.

3.

6.

7.

9.

10.

Down

2.

4.

5.

8.

UNIT 2 *Wordsearch*

```
T  N  M  O  T  H  E  R  O  S  M  U  P  L  F  I  G  V
U  V  U  V  J  M  Y  N  M  H  W  P  A  U  R  W  R  D
E  M  T  H  U  R  S  D  A  Y  H  J  C  P  I  E  A  N
S  K  S  S  A  T  U  R  D  A  Y  J  H  D  D  D  N  S
D  D  P  L  O  Z  I  L  U  E  D  N  I  M  A  N  D  E
A  E  O  L  J  O  M  E  H  J  P  V  L  G  Y  E  F  J
Y  K  U  U  H  U  S  B  A  N  D  Z  D  I  D  S  A  S
A  A  S  K  M  O  N  D  A  Y  O  O  R  D  G  D  T  K
K  D  E  B (B  R  O  T  H  E  R) C  E  A  M  A  H  X
M  X  N  U  K  O  N  E  Q  O  W  S  N  U  P  Y  E  T
Z  T  Q  R  Z  C  W  D  U  Z  E  I  W  G  P  B  R  A
U  G  U  V  T  A  S  F  A  M  I  L  Y  H  V  O  W  S
O  W  F  A  T  H  E  R  R  T  H  R  T  T  S  O  N  U
Z  G  Y  I  N  C  N  Y  U  C  Q  B  M  E  N  A  B  N
S  F  E  W  D  C  C  P  V  A  N  X  K  R  V  P  Z  D
G  Y  T  W  F  E  Y  Y  K  S  W  O  L  Q  U  O  D  A
W  G  R  A  N  D  M  O  T  H  E  R  Y  Y  Y  Q  N  Y
N  W  I  F  E  S  I  S  T  E  R  D  Z  V  T  H  N  S
```

✔ __ BROTHER   __ GRANDMOTHER   __ SPOUSE

__ CHILDREN   __ HUSBAND   ✔ __ SUNDAY

__ DAUGHTER   __ MONDAY   __ THURSDAY

__ FAMILY   __ MOTHER   __ TUESDAY

__ FATHER   __ SATURDAY   __ WEDNESDAY

__ FRIDAY   __ SISTER   __ WIFE

__ GRANDFATHER   __ SON

Can we buy some ice cream?

Ice Cream

Ice cream, ice cream
we all scream
for
ice cream.

Chocolate, vanilla, strawberry
Lemon, lime and cherry.

Ice cream, ice cream
we all dream
of
ice cream.

What good is food shopping?

What good is food shopping if we eat it all up?
We bring it all home
then
cup by cup
we
eat the beans, the peas, the rice
and
go
back
for more
at twice the price.

Maybe the food on the shelf we should keep
at least for a day or a week.
Our trips to the store might become less and less
but
our lives would be easier, not as much stress.

Where's the food?

 A. Read the words.

1. **Fruits**   **Vegetables**
oranges   beans
apples   cabbage
bananas   carrots
peaches   broccoli
potatoes

2. **Frozen foods**
ice cream
juice

3. **Baking Goods**
flour
sugar
salt

4. **Meats, Poultry, Fish**
chicken
beef
fish
pork

5. **Dairy Products**
milk
butter

6. **Rice/ Noodles**
rice
noodles
pasta

7. **Beverages**
soda
coffee
tea

8. **Bakery**
cake
cookies
bread

 B. Write the word under the picture.

1. *bananas*   2. _____   3. _____   4. _____

5. _____   6. _____   7. _____   8. _____

9. _____   10. _____   11. _____   12. _____

13. _____   14. _____   15. _____   16. _____

Fruits and vegetables from my country.

A. My country is _____.

B. Draw pictures of two different fruits from your country.
Write their names.

This is a _____.   This is a _____.

C. Draw pictures of two different vegetables from your country.
Write their names.

This is a _____.   This is a _____.

D. Share your pictures with your classmates.

What's your favorite fruit?

A. Ask 9 students these questions. Write their answers in the chart.

What's your favorite fruit?   *What's your favorite vegetable?*

What's your favorite meat?   *What others do you like? Add them to the list.*

Name	Fruits	Vegetables	Meats, Poultry, Fish
	oranges	beans	chicken
	apples	cabbage	beef
	bananas	carrots	fish
	peaches	broccoli	pork
		potatoes	

1. _____ _____ _____ _____
   (your name)

2. _____ _____ _____ _____

3. _____ _____ _____ _____

4. _____ _____ _____ _____

5. _____ _____ _____ _____

6. _____ _____ _____ _____

7. _____ _____ _____ _____

8. _____ _____ _____ _____

9. _____ _____ _____ _____

10. _____ _____ _____ _____

B. Count the favorite items. Complete the sentences.

_____ is the fruit my friends like best.

_____ is the vegetable my friends like best.

_____ is the meat my friends like best.

What's the total?

Add the amount. Draw the money.

1. *Duttonville Market*

bread	$ 1.02
milk	1.76
pasta	1.21
total	**$ 3.99**

2. *ABC Market*

bread	$ .94
milk	1.03
pasta	2.01
total	**$**

3. *Speedy Mart*

bread	$ 1.19
milk	1.60
pasta	2.21
total	**$**

4. *JOHNSON'S MARKET*

bread	$ .94
milk	1.13
pasta	1.81
total	**$**

5. *SUPER Supermarket*

bread	$ .72
milk	1.01
pasta	1.27
total	**$**

Can you figure out the change?

What I want to buy	The money I have	The change I will get back
3 oranges $ .76		$ \begin{array}{r} \$1.00 \\ -\ .76 \\ \hline \$.24 \end{array} $
bunch of bananas $1.82		
a whole chicken $3.90		
fish $6.76		
two steaks $8.87		
a cake $18.98		

| ¹P | E | A | ²C | H | E | S | | ³ |

Across

1.

5.

6.

7.

9.

11.

bananas
bread
broccoli
cabbage
cake
carrots
cookies
fish
oranges
peaches
potatoes
rice

Down

1.

2.

3.

4.

8.

10.

UNIT 3 Wordsearch

```
C A W H R D A N C D O C W F N N J Z J J H D C S U
U N F C S E T L M P K S N S O D S O I D D B L U T
T S U N Z O D Q A L B F V Y M R H Y I A M L I X V
N T A C Z N P I L A G C C J O K U G L Y P S J J E
S L M K K Y N Q M Q I T M U N E Y Y V N P H Y N Z N
O S W B J J Q L D L Y T M H E P N D Q O W Y L V N
D F U I I B X K Y F T K F V Y Q M X N U T P L D G
A L B R E A D C J I N A B W I B E E F P J S V Q P
M O J Z O N W O W S Q E F J K L J G U D D E G O K
V U T E U V M O W H Q U A R T E R P A L F L K M X
L R C T D I K K V D Y X F U V Y A H H U X Z O P T
V Y J D R W K I E Z Z B E B B P L J Q F W R G H L
V C V I R B N E J X P R Q M S O P E B R W S H R E
A O Z M W C U S T A T Q N A U R E C Z Y W R L V U
V F S E B U T T E R F C H I C K E N F W V X Z L C
V F J C Q T W P F N D C T K Q E Z N I C K E L F W
R E Q Q Y D G P B O C T G D M W C Y I J X M C N P
M E I K T T X D B O L F N M Q H P V D N M O L R J
E P B S U L R D N D D B R J W S C G B M M E K Q D
I A R L E C I X F L H M B E X R C A L P W A W G
W S V T T J C G H E D R L F X X S V R Y E P S B W
V T O O H E E H L S S X I E A L N B S V N J U T D
D A T J D S U G A R O D A R D O L L A R N C C M A
Y K W W P Y B G H F H M H V B G T Z Q M Y S O W J
D D R K U V Z U T B D O R N U O Y X Q R Z D A A R
```

___ **BEEF**	___ **BREAD**	✔ **BUTTER**	___ **COOKIES**
___ **CHICKEN**	___ **FISH**	___ **NOODLES**	___ **PORK**
___ **RICE**	___ **SUGAR**	✔ **FLOUR**	___ **COFFEE**
___ **SODA**	___ **PENNY**	___ **NICKEL**	___ **DIME**
___ **QUARTER**	___ **DOLLAR**	___ **MONEY**	___ **PASTA**

UNIT 4

Can you identify items in this kitchen?

 A. Identify each item in the picture above. Write the number in the circle.

1. cabinet   **2.** floor   **3.** curtain   **4.** door

cabinet _____   _____   _____   _____

5. microwave   **6.** refrigerator   **7.** shelf   **8.** sink

_____   _____   _____   _____

9. stove   **10.** table   **11.** window

_____   _____   _____

B. Read each word, then write it.

What's in your kitchen?

A. Draw a picture of your kitchen at home.

B. Write a list of things you have in your kitchen.
Ask your teacher for help with new words.

What's in the house?

 A. Put these items in the rooms of the house. Write the words.

chest	microwave	TV	stove	table
chairs	closet	bed	lamps	shower
picture	sofa	mirror	refrigerator	curtains
stove	bed	tub	cabinet	sink

Living Room	Bedroom	Bathroom	Kitchen

 B. What other furniture do you have in your house? Add those items to the list.

Who's doing what? Where?

Look at the picture.
Read the story on page 41 to help you write the sentence.

1. _____ Grandpa is reading a book. _____

2. _____

3. _____

4. _____

5. _____

6. _____

28

Cooking chicken in the kitchen

Cooking chicken in the kitchen
It's my favorite thing to do.
I pop it in the pot
and make a yummy stew.

I slip the bird into the pot
Add onions, carrots, too.
I use my mother's secret spice
To make this stew for you.

Come over to my kitchen
Visit while I cook
We'll sip a cup of coffee
Lift up the lid to take a look.

This scent of cooking chicken
Fills the house with such good smell
That cooking chicken in the kitchen
Turns out so very well.

Color My Balloon

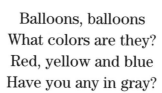

Balloons, balloons
What colors are they?
Red, yellow and blue
Have you any in gray?

Purple and pinkish
Orange, green and light brown
White, black, and navy
They certainly are round.

How many, how many
Balloons do you see?
Count them and save one
Just for me, me.

What's your favorite color?

 A. **Read the color words. Color the balloons.**

| red | yellow | blue | green | purple | orange |

 B. **Ask your friends this question. Write the answer in the chart.**

What's your favorite color?   It's _____.

Name	Favorite color
1. *(your name)*	
2.	
3.	
4.	
5.	
6.	

C. **Write about you.**

My favorite color is _____.

D. **Look at the chart and finish this sentence.**

_____ is the color my friends like best.

UNIT 4 Crossword Puzzle

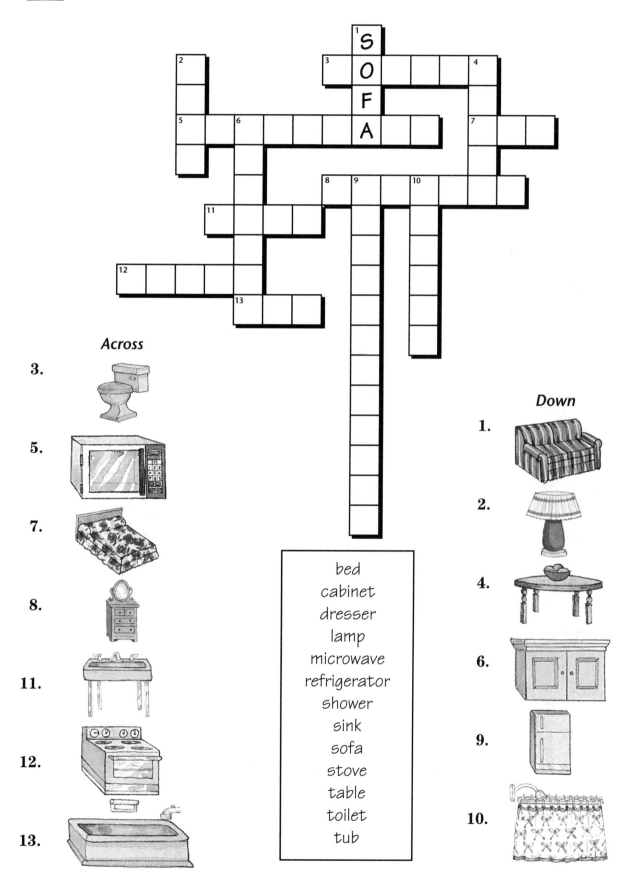

Across

3.

5.

7.

8.

11.

12.

13.

bed
cabinet
dresser
lamp
microwave
refrigerator
shower
sink
sofa
stove
table
toilet
tub

Down

1.

2.

4.

6.

9.

10.

UNIT 4 *Wordsearch*

```
J  Q  D  H  U  L  H  Z  R  E  D  P  N  R
Y  K  D  R  T  P  W  B  H  B  D  O  G  E
Z  N  Y  B  U  E  E  O  E  U  D  J  Q  F
Q  M  R  D  T  H  P  E  L  U  N  U  B  R
W  P  U  R  P  L  E  Y  E  L  L  O  W  I
C  K  Z  T  U  B  Y  D  V  F  K  X  L  G
A  I  K  M  D  S  X  C  S  Z  R  S  R  E
B  T  L  N  I  H  S  L  H  F  T  H  G  R
I  C  S  B  V  O  T  O  D  F  Y  E  R  A
N  H  I  L  V  W  O  S  N  U  E  L  E  T
E  E  N  U  P  E  V  E  C  J  I  F  E  O
T  N  K  X  I  R  E  T  U  A  Z  H  N  R
C  I  Y  B  V  B  A  T  H  R  O  O  M  T
C  G  W  E  B  L  U  E  O  I  Y  Y  H  I
```

___ **CABINET**   ___ **YELLOW**   ___ **RED**

___ **TUB**   ___ **BATHROOM**   ___ **PURPLE**

___ **CLOSET**   ___ **SHOWER**   ___ **REFRIGERATOR**

___ **KITCHEN**   ___ **SINK**   ___ **SHELF**

___ **GREEN**   ✓ **STOVE**   ✓ **BLUE**

I like shopping at Dutton's Department Store.

A. Read the words.

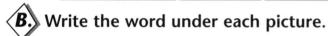

a dress	a coat	underwear	a suit
a blouse	a purse	a hat	a sweater
pants	socks	a cap	a tie
a T–shirt	sandals	shorts	tennis shoes

B. Write the word under each picture.

1. _shorts_   2. _____   3. _____   4. _____

5. _____   6. _____   7. _____   8. _____

9. _____   10. _____   11. _____   12. _____

13. _____   14. _____   15. _____   16. _____

Let's look back.

Look on page 49. What are the people at Dutton's Department Store wearing? Read and complete the sentences.

It is a ___red___ dress.

Makeba is wearing a ___red___ ___dress___.

The sandals are black.

They are ___black___ sandals.

She is ___wearing___ black ___sandals___.

The dress is blue.

It is a _____ dress.

Petra is wearing a _____ _____.

The shoes are brown

They are _____ shoes.

She is _____ brown _____.

The suit is blue.

It is a _____ suit.

Hiroshi is _____ a _____ _____.

The shoes are black.

They are _____ _____.

He is _____ _____ _____.

Everything is 50% off!

Are you having a sale?

Yes! Everything is 50% off!

	a sweater $11.90	a pair of socks $.60	a coat $25.00	a suit $60.40	a pair of pants $8.50	a hat $4.32	a pair of shorts $6.85
Kim		X	X		X		
Rose					X		X
Ali		X		X			
José				X			X
Carmen	X	X					
Carlos			X			X	
Bic			X	X	X		
Hiroshi	X		X	X	X		

A. Complete each sentence, using the information above.

1. Kim is buying _____SOCKS_____, _____ and _____.

2. José is buying _____ and _____.

3. Bic is buying _____, _____ and _____.

4. Hiroshi is buying _____, _____, _____, and

   _____.

B. Write the answers.

a. Who is buying socks and a sweater? _____

b. Who is buying a coat and a hat? _____

c. Who is buying pants and shorts? _____

d. Who is buying a suit and socks? _____

35

Do you get any change?

Dutton's Department Store
SALE!

	$11.90
	$6.84
TOTAL	$ 28.74
cash	30.00
change	$1.26

Thank you!

Look at the chart on page 35. Write the answers.

1. Rose

Rose is buying

a pair of pants

and a pair of

shorts.

Here is her receipt.

DUTTON'S DEPARTMENT STORE	
pants	$8.50
shorts	*6.85*
TOTAL	*15.35*
cash	$20.00
change	$ *4.65*
Thank you	

2. Carmen

Carmen is buying

_____

_____

_____

Here is her receipt.

DUTTON'S DEPARTMENT STORE	
_____	_____
_____	_____
TOTAL	_____
cash	$15.00
change	$ _____
Thank you	

3. Hiroshi

_____

_____

_____

Here is his receipt.

DUTTON'S DEPARTMENT STORE	
_____	_____
_____	_____
_____	_____
TOTAL	_____
cash	$120.00
change	$ _____
Thank you	

Small, medium or large?

A. Draw a line.

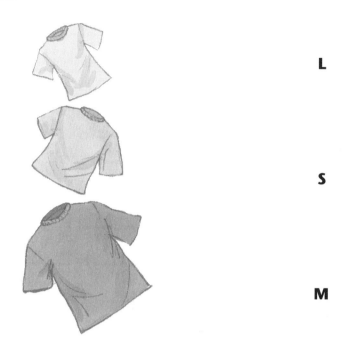

L

S

M

What month is it?

B. Complete the crossword puzzle with the months of the year.

April	August	December	February	January	July
June	March	May	November	October	September

The Price is Right.

The price is right. No need to fight.

It fits great! Not too tight!

Do you have three in all sizes?

Let's go look–no surprises.

Here they are–large, medium and small.

Enough for you and your family, all.

A. **What about you?**

My birthday is on _____ _____ .

　　　　　　　　　　month　　　　　　　　day

B. **What do you want for your birthday?**
Draw a picture of what you want for your birthday.

UNIT 5 Crossword Puzzle

Across

1.
3.
4.
5.
7.
8.
10.
11.
12.

blouse
cap
coat
dress
pants
sandals
shirt
shoes
shorts
skirt
socks
suit
sweater
tie
underwear

Down

1.
2.
3.
6.
7.
9.

UNIT 5 Wordsearch

```
B  C  Y  B  D  L  O  H  L  B  U  V  I  S
D  L  C  T  I  E  U  R  L  O  X  U  K  C
R  S  A  V  V  P  N  C  V  V  K  M  T  G
E  A  P  T  X  U  D  O  P  O  V  N  H  L
S  N  K  C  M  R  E  A  G  C  V  Z  S  P
S  D  Q  D  P  S  R  T  A  P  Q  K  H  S
F  A  E  F  R  E  W  G  F  P  E  S  O  U
S  L  S  G  I  H  E  X  U  P  E  N  R  I
X  S  K  R  S  A  A  Q  N  X  E  A  T  T
H  O  I  E  I  T  R  P  C  Y  S  H  S  B
P  C  R  P  A  N  T  S  P  M  M  B  R  Q
O  K  T  N  J  I  S  N  T  G  V  A  D  E
L  S  S  W  E  A  T  E  R  W  T  H  T  D
L  N  S  H  I  R  T  B  L  O  U  S  E  R
```

___ UNDERWEAR   ___ DRESS   ___ PANTS   ✔ COAT

___ PURSE   ___ SOCKS   ___ SANDALS   ___ HAT

___ SHIRT   ___ SHORTS   ___ SUIT   ___ SWEATER

___ TIE   ✔ BLOUSE   ___ CAP   ___ SKIRT

Where do you want to go?

A. Read the words.

1. library
2. school
3. bank

4. market
5. post office
6. movie theater

7. church
8. park
9. hospital

B. Write the word under the picture.

a. _____park_____

b. _____

c. _____

d. _____

e. _____

f. _____

g. _____

h. _____

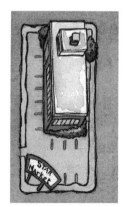

i. _____

What can you find at a yard sale?

A. Read the words.

1. pots and pans	5. tea kettle	9. broom	13. glasses
2. washer	6. iron	10. toaster	14. dishes
3. ironing board	7. tie	11. vacuum	15. lamps
4. coffee pot	8. rocking chair	12. books	16. blouses

 B. Write the words under the picture.

a. *pots and pans* b. _____ c. _____ d. _____

e. _____ f. _____ g. _____ h. _____

i. _____ j. _____ k. _____ l. _____

m. _____ n. _____ o. _____ p. _____

What do you want to buy at the yard sale?

1. pots and pans
2. washer
3. ironing board
4. coffee pot
5. table
6. tea kettle
7. dryer
8. iron
9. ties
10. chairs
11. broom
12. toaster
13. vacuum
14. books
15. dresses
16. glasses
17. dishes
18. trash can
19. lamps
20. blouses

What do you want to buy at the yard sale?

I want to buy _____ and _____.

 A. Interview your classmates. Write what they want to buy. They may buy only two things.

Name	item number 1	item number 2
1.		
2.		
3.		
4.		
5.		
6.		
7.		

B. Look at your chart. Complete the sentence.

_____ and _____ are the two things

my friends like the best.

Can you find the place?

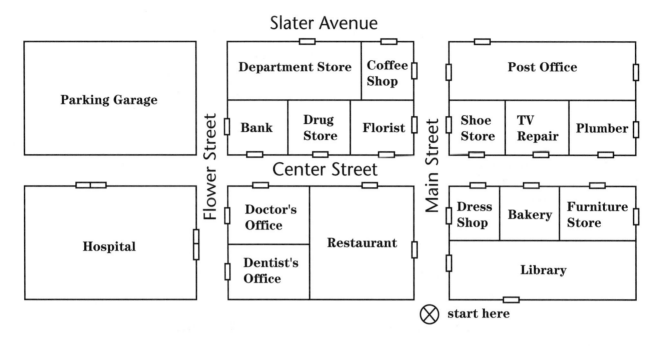

Slater Avenue

Parking Garage		Department Store	Coffee Shop		Post Office	

Flower Street

| Bank | Drug Store | Florist | | Shoe Store | TV Repair | Plumber |

Center Street

Main Street

| Hospital | | Doctor's Office | | Restaurant | | Dress Shop | Bakery | Furniture Store |
| Dentist's Office | | | Library |

⊗ start here

Look at the map. Answer the questions.

1. Go straight on Main Street for 1 block and go left on Center Street. Enter the first door on the left.

   You are at the _____**restaurant**_____ .

2. Walk north or straight ahead on Main Street to Slater Avenue. Go left on Slater. Enter the second door on your left.

   You are at the _____ .

3. Across the street from the hospital on Center Street is the _____ .

4. On Center Street, the _____ is between the bank and the florist shop.

5. The florist shop is on the corner of _____ and _____ .

6. The TV Repair is on _____ between the _____

   and the _____ .

7. Go straight on Main Street and go right on Center Street. Enter the second building on your right.

   You are at the _____ .

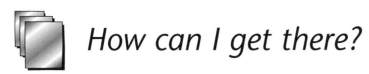

How can I get there?

How can I get there?

How can I get there?
Do I go left or right?

Do I walk to the corner?
Shall I turn at the light?

Do I walk close beside it?
Do I run in between?
Oh, thanks for the map
I see what you mean.

Draw a map of where you live and your neighborhood.

Where is the nearest market? My address is _____.

Our yard sale in class.

A. Draw pictures of four items you want to bring from home to sell at a yard sale.

B. Write a price for each item.

C. Write your name on each item card.

D. Cut out the cards. Place all class cards together to form the class yard sale. Have fun buying and selling the class items.

E. Use this conversation to help you bargain for the items.

> **A:** I see you want $_____ for this _____.
>
> Will you take $_____ instead?
>
> **B:** How about $_____?
>
> **A:** That's a deal. You've just made a sale.

UNIT 6 Crossword Puzzle

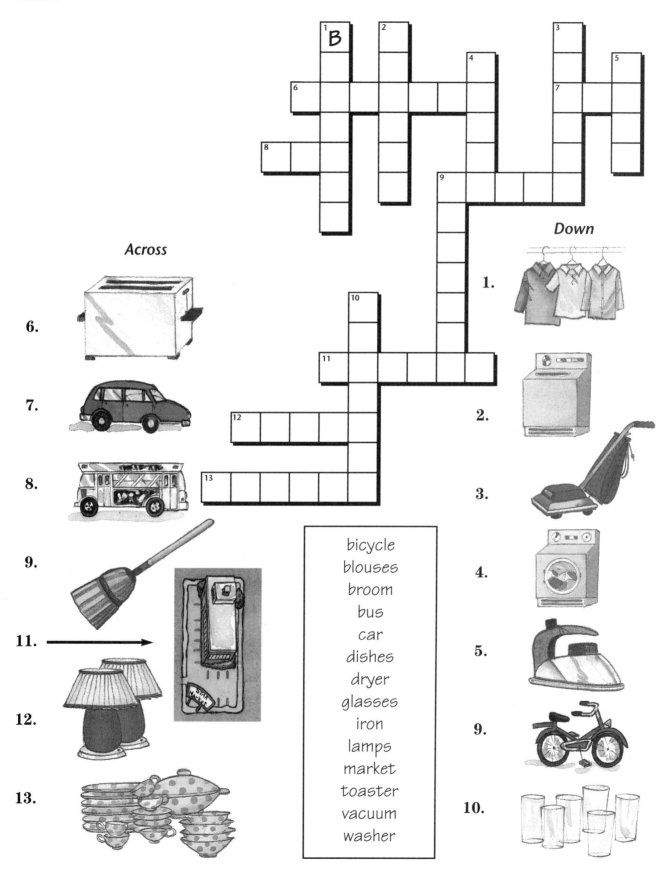

Across

6.

7.

8.

9.

11.

12.

13.

Down

1.

2.

3.

4.

5.

9.

10.

bicycle
blouses
broom
bus
car
dishes
dryer
glasses
iron
lamps
market
toaster
vacuum
washer

UNIT 6 Wordsearch

```
H  S  G  O  M  F  K  E  R  S  Z  I  H  R  S  R  P  K  F  O
C  O  B  P  G  C  I  A  A  L  J  B  J  V  P  X  Z  G  Z  U
I  H  R  N  K  H  Q  P  A (C  L  O  T  H  I  N  G) Y  H  H
K  D  X  T  K  U  H  P  B  J  U  T  B  Z  Y  P  I  Y  R  X
D  G  C  V  E  R  M  L  A  D  R  W  Z  S  M  S  P  M  H  V
R  T  E  K  H  C  U  I  N  T  I  M  U  B  Q  N  V  X  C  Q
I  Z  N  W  S  H  D  A  K  V  G  J  Y  U  P  O  I  M  F  P
F  J  V  I  A  Q  K  N  J  L  H  R  W  R  K  P  T  F  U  H
Q  U  U  N  E  T  F  C  Y  Y  T  V  S  S  C  H  O  O  L  V
L  A  E  U  S  H  E  E  W  F  G  N  Z  V  F  R  E  L  A  B
X  U  E  H  H  E  L  S  F  X  A  M  W  N  F  F  C  N  A  R
B  J  D  T  G  A  P (A  M  Q  R  F  S  T  R  E  E  T  C  X
E  X  P  A  I  T  W  V) A  O  A  J  M  C  E  Q  E  X  R  P
S  P  M  L  H  E  C  E) R  Y  G  D  U  O  V  I  E  X  O  W
I  G  O  F  Y  R  M  N) K  W  E  S  Y  R  E  K  O  S  S  W
D  I  J  R  K  P  T  U) E  Z  T  A  P  N  L  I  W  M  S  K
E  K  T  Y  Q  A  J  E) T  K  S  T  B  E  E  M  O  X  E  Z
R  Q  P  L  S  R  O  I  L  V  Z  R  K  R  F  H  A  E  C  U
J  I  X  O  B  K  G  M  Z  U  H  I  Y  C  T  K  M  R  F  C
L  L  A  T  D  J  Q  B  J  H  Y  J  O  S  R  P  R  V  T  Q
```

___ SCHOOL   ___ PARK   ___ CORNER   ___ CHURCH

___ MARKET   ___ THEATER   ___ BANK   ___ GARAGE

___ BESIDE   ___ ACROSS   ✓ AVENUE   ___ STREET

___ RIGHT   ___ LEFT   ___ APPLIANCES   ✓ CLOTHING

What's the emergency?

Look at the picture. Write the missing word.

1.

I cut my leg.

It's _____ *bleeding* _____.

2.

Help!

There's a _____ at the bank.

3.

Look! That house is on

_____.

4.

Help! Let's get that man out of the ocean.

I think he is _____.

5.

Emergency! The car hit the man. Get help!

There's a traffic _____.

6.

Look at that woman!

Is she _____?

How's the weather?

Write the missing word under the picture.

1. cloudy   **3.** cold   **5.** foggy   **7.** hot

2. raining   **4.** snowing   **6.** sunny   **8.** windy

a. It is ____*cold*____ today.

b. It is _____ today.

c. It is _____ today.

d. It is _____ today.

e. It is _____ today.

f. It is _____ today.

g. It is _____ today.

h. It is _____ today.

Do you like it when it's cold?

Do you like it when it's cold?   Yes, I do.

No, I don't.

1. cloudy   3. cold   5. foggy   7. hot
2. raining   4. snowing   6. sunny   8. windy

A. Find out about your classmates.
Interview your classmates and fill in this chart. Write **X** for *Yes*.

Do you like it when it's _____ *cloudy* _____?

Name	cloudy	raining	cold	snowing	foggy	sunny	hot	windy
Kay			X	X		X		X

B. Look at the chart and complete the sentences.

Many classmates like it when it's _____.

Many classmates don't like it when it's _____.

Going to the emergency room.

 A. Read the words.

1. ambulance   3. doctors   5. emergency room   7. hospital

2. medical form   4. nurses   6. paramedics   8. patient

 B. Look at each picture and complete the sentence.

a. The ____*ambulance*____ is going to the hospital.

b. The _____ are helping Carlos.

c. Carlos is in the _____.

d. Carlos is now a _____.

e. The ambulance takes Carlos to the _____.

f. The _____ are examining Carlos.

g. The _____ are helping the doctor.

h. Who is completing the _____?

What's the matter?

What's the matter?

His arm is hurt.

A. Read the words.

1. arm
2. back
3. chest
4. foot
5. hand
6. head
7. leg
8. neck

B. Write the word under the picture.

a. _____

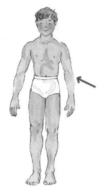

b. _____

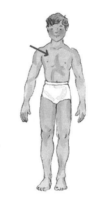

c. _____

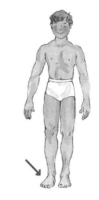

d. _____

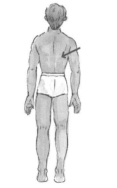

e. _____

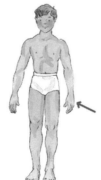

f. _____

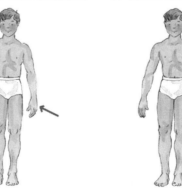

g. _____

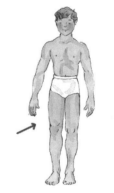

h. _____

Body Parts

Arms and legs and neck and chest
What part of your body do you like the best?

Of all my parts, I like my head.
Because if I lose it, I'll be dead.

53

Tell me again.

A. What happened first? What happened next?
Write the numbers 1 to 5. Put the sentences in the correct order.

_____ The ambulance takes Carlos to the emergency room.

_____ A car hits Carlos.

__1__ Carlos is crossing the street.

_____ The doctor and nurse examine Carlos.

_____ Jose calls 911.

B. Write the story.

Carlos _____

_____

_____

_____

_____

Across

2.

4.

6.

7.

8.

9.

10.

Down

1.

3.

4.

5.

7.

bleeding
choking
cloudy
cold
drowning
foggy
hot
raining
robbery
snowing
sunny
windy

UNIT 7   Wordsearch

```
A  B  L  H  O  S  P  I  T  A  L  F  F  F
C  X  W  E  B  A  A  R  J  B  L  D  O  H
C  L  C  M  L  V  D  O  C  T  O  R  O  Q
I  E  A  E  E  D  F  B  B  R  K  O  T  I
D  G  M  R  E  O  C  B  V  F  U  W  A  F
E  Q  B  G  D  V  R  E  Q  M  A  N  X  J
N  V  U  E  I  G  L  R  Z  D  G  I  L  K
T  O  L  N  N  E  L  Y  Z  U  A  N  U  D
A  E  A  C  G  I  E  X  F  O  G  G  U  W
R  H  N  Y  Y  H  T  F  I  R  E  A  H  E
M  F  C  G  N  U  R  S  E  X  F  L  E  G
F  S  E  K  C  H  O  K  I  N  G  F  A  Z
X  B  A  C  K  G  D  O  C  T  O  R  D  A
P  A  R  A  M  E  D  I  C  Z  D  Q  E  K
```

___ ACCIDENT	___ AMBULANCE	✓ ARM	___ BLEEDING
___ CHOKING	___ DOCTOR	___ PARAMEDIC	___ ROBBERY
___ DROWNING	___ EMERGENCY	✓ FIRE	___ FOOT
___ HEAD	___ HOSPITAL	___ NURSE	___ DOCTOR
___ BACK	___ LEG		

Health Information Form.

Patient Information Form

Name _____

             last   first   middle initial

Address _____

            number   street   apartment #

_____

            city   state   zip code

Date of birth _____ Age _____ Male _____ Female _____

            month - date - year

Who can we call in case of an emergency?

Name _____ Phone _____

Relationship _____

- -

Do you have problems with:

_____ cold   _____ headache   _____ stomachache

_____ cough   _____ fever   _____ earache

_____ sore throat   _____ backache

_____ toothache   _____ other (Write here.) _____

- -

Are you taking any kind of medicine now?   _____ Yes   _____ No

What kind of medicine? _____

- -

If the patient is a minor, please sign.

Signature _____ Date _____

Relationship to patient _____

What's the matter?

Look at the picture. Complete the sentence.

1.

Ali has a _____ *fever* _____.

Ali has a fever. _____

2.

Carlos is _____.

_____

3.

Carmen has a _____.

_____

4.

Petra has a _____.

_____

5.

Hiroshi has a _____.

_____

What hurts?

Look at the picture. Write the missing word. Then write the sentence.

1.

Van's _____ *back* _____ hurts.

Van's back hurts.

2.

Makeba's _____ hurts.

_____

3.

Charlie's _____ hurts.

_____

4.

Bic's _____ hurts.

_____

5.

Pedro's _____ hurts.

_____

6.

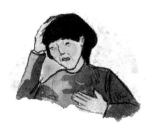

Rose's _____ hurts.

_____

Where do I put the cold remedies?

Read the directions and put the cold remedies away.
Write the letter on the line in the medicine cabinet.

A.

B.

C.

D.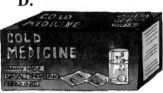

E.

F.

G.

H.

Directions:
1. **aspirin**–top shelf on the left
2. **pills**–middle shelf in the middle
3. **cough syrup**–top shelf in the middle
4. **cold medicine**–bottom shelf to the right
5. **bowl of chicken soup**–table to the left
6. **nose drops**–top shelf to the right
7. **ear drops**–bottom shelf to the left
8. **cup of hot tea**–table to the right

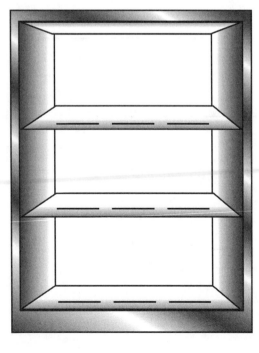

What do you do every day?
What does Carlos do every day?

Look at the pictures and complete the sentences.

I _____**shower**_____ every day.

Carlos _____**showers**_____ every day.

shower   showers

I _____**rest**_____ on Saturdays and
Sundays.

Pedro _____ on Saturdays
and Sundays.

rest   rests

I _____ daily.

Carlos _____ daily.

exercise   exercises

I _____ fruits and
vegetables every day.

Carlos _____ fruits and
vegetables every day.

eat   eats

What do you do every day?
What does Carlos do every day?

I _____ eight hours every
night.

Carlos _____ eight hours
every night.

sleep   sleeps

I _____ my teeth everyday.

Carlos _____ his teeth
every day.

brush   brushes

Staying Healthy

What do you do to stay so well?

I exercise every day, can't you tell?

I rest, and I brush,

I sleep, and I shower,

I eat lots of fruit

That gives me great power.

UNIT 8 Crossword Puzzle

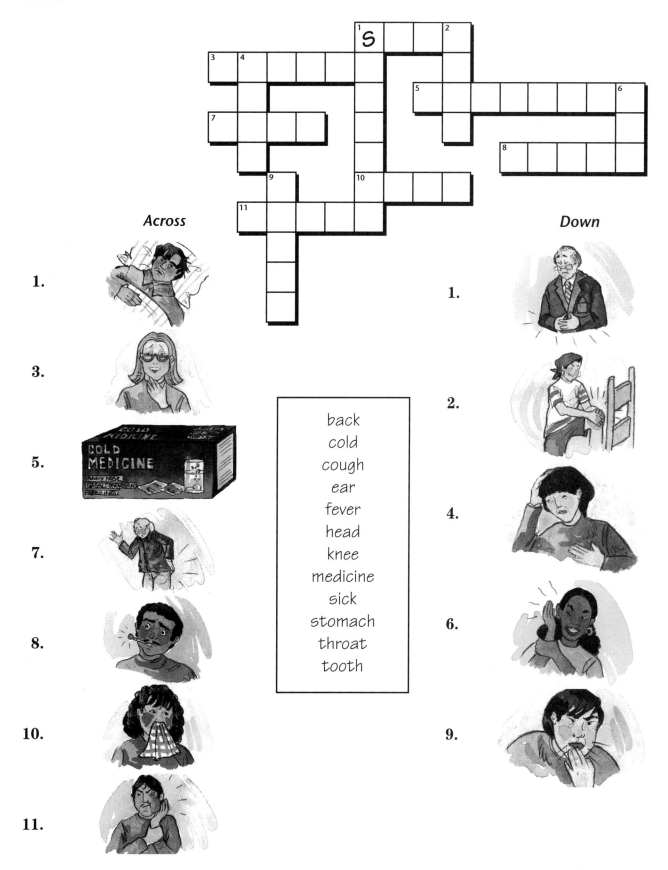

Across

1.

3.

5.

7.

8.

10.

11.

back
cold
cough
ear
fever
head
knee
medicine
sick
stomach
throat
tooth

Down

1.

2.

4.

6.

9.

UNIT 8 Wordsearch

```
A  O  H  B  D  R  N  S  K  N  A  P  N  R  V  V
C  H  N  Y  S  S  S  Y  S  H  S  I  L  P  G  K
O  E  B  T  M  W  O  R  L  C  P  U  T  S  U  X
L  A  K  E  T  P  R  U  E  B  I  A  O  P  U  V
D  L  H  P  H  Q  E  P  E  E  R  F  O  P  V  P
G  T  X  E  Y  C  G  N  P  S  I  X  T  L  O  I
R  H  L  R  C  O  U  G  H  I  N  G  H  D  S  U
E  Y  T  L  Q  S  R  Z  C  O  I  U  R  O  Y  A
V  D  M  D  Q  D  R  O  P  S  T  V  R  Z  I  G
S  H  O  W  E  R  O  Q  R  U  G  U  I  J  E  M
Y  B  R  U  S  H  I  F  E  V  E  R  G  S  T  U
H  O  P  L  Z  U  X  M  S  T  R  Q  G  R  L  P
L  K  K  P  L  T  W  Z  T  C  H  L  R  U  Z  R
E  X  E  R  C  I  S  E  C  E  A  T  Y  B  S  O
C  J  Q  R  R  I  G  L  Q  P  F  I  Y  U  L  I
B  T  A  M  E  D  I  C  I  N  E  E  Q  K  I  B
```

___ **SLEEP**   ___ **EAT**   ___ **EXERCISE**   ___ **BRUSH**

___ **TOOTH**   ___ **REST**   ___ **SHOWER**   ___ **HEALTHY**

___ **MEDICINE**   ___ **ASPIRIN**   ✔ **SYRUP**   ___ **COUGH**

✔ **DROPS**   ___ **FEVER**   ___ **COLD**   ___ **SORE**

Watch out for the cars!

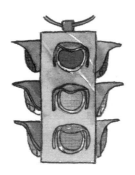

red = Stop!

yellow = Caution! Be Careful!

green = Go!

A. Read.

1. Walk here.
2. Go out here!
3. Stop! School children crossing.

4. The traffic light is red, yellow, and green.
5. Don't turn left.
6. Stop your car!

7. Don't park here!
8. Don't go there.
9. Don't turn right!

B. Write the sentence under the picture.

a. _____

b. _____

c. _____

d. _____

e. _____

f. _____

g. _____

h. _____

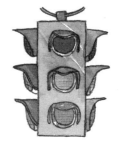

i. _____

How do you come to school?

Read the words. Draw a line to the correct picture. Write the words under the picture.

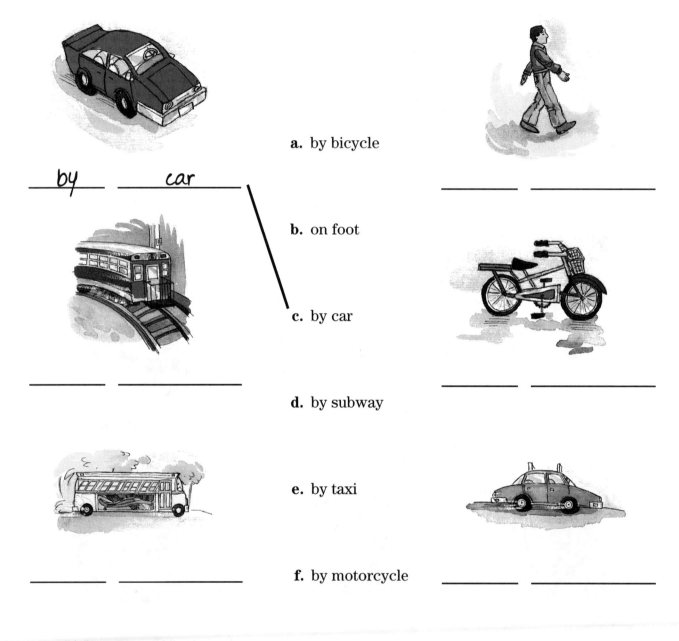

_by_   _car_

a. by bicycle

b. on foot

c. by car

d. by subway

e. by taxi

f. by motorcycle

g. by bus

How do you come to school?

How do you come to school?   How does he come to school?

I <u>come</u> by bus.	He She } <u>comes</u> by bus.

A. Look at the information on page 101. Complete the sentence.
Then write the complete sentence.

1. Van ____*comes*____ to school ___*by*___ _____*bus*_____ every day.

   __Van comes to school by bus every day._____.

2. Carlos _____ to school _____ _____ every day.

   _____.

B. Now write about you and your friends.

1. _____ _____ to school _____ _____ every day.

   _____.

2. _____ _____ to school _____ _____ every day.

   _____.

3. _____ _____ to school _____ _____ every day.

   _____.

How do you come to school?

4. _____ _____ to school _____ _____ every day.

_____.

5. _____ _____ to school _____ _____ every day.

_____.

6. _____ _____ to school _____ _____ every day.

_____.

7. _____ _____ to school _____ _____ every day.

_____.

8. _____ _____ to school _____ _____ every day.

_____.

9. _____I_____ ____come____ to school _____ _____ every day.

_____.

10. _My teacher_ _comes_ to school _____ _____ every day.

_____.

Where should you go?
Who should you call?

A. **Read the words.**

a. restaurant
b. laundromat
c. movie theater
d. the police

e. fire department
f. department store
g. bakery
h. gas station

i. drug store
j. library
k. post office
l. Department of Motor Vehicles

B. **Read and write the letter.**
Where do you go?   Who do you call?

___f___ **1.** Where do you go to buy a dress?

_____ **2.** Where do you go to see a movie?

_____ **3.** Where do you go to buy some gas?

_____ **4.** Where do you go to buy a doughnut?

_____ **5.** Where do you go to wash your clothes?

_____ **6.** Where do you go to send a letter?

_____ **7.** Where do you go to buy some pills for a headache?

_____ **8.** Who do you call to report a fire?

_____ **9.** Who do you call to report a robbery?

_____ **10.** Where do you go to get a driver's license?

_____ **11.** Where do you go to read a book?

_____ **12.** Where do you go to eat some food?

C. **About you. Read and answer the question.**

Where do you go to learn English?

I _____ to _____ to learn English.

D. **Write the sentence.**

_____

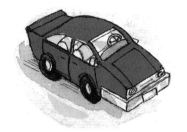

HOW DO YOU TRAVEL?

How do you travel?
How do you go?
By car or by bus?
On foot, very slow?

Can you get there by subway?
Will a bike ride do?
Wow! I see your Harley
All shiny and new.

GREEN LIGHT, RED LIGHT

Around the corner, up the street,
Turn right, turn left,
Hey, watch your feet.

Green light, red light,
Yellow, too.
Watch all the signs
'Cause they help you.

UNIT 9 Crossword Puzzle

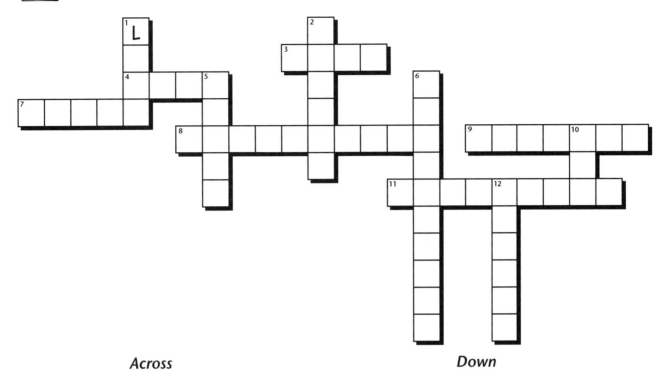

Across

3.

4.

7.

8.

9.

11.

Down

1.

2.

5.

6.

10.

12.

bakery	foot	right
bicycle	laundromat	subway
car	left	taxi
drugstore	motorcycle	train

UNIT 9 Wordsearch

```
J O X Q R E S T A U R A N T J D E
X Z A G D Y Z B R K C S V G H U E
O H W A S F Z U V G Y C E X U S J
C G I G A L X S B Y S H H L D C F
Q S T A T I O N J M X E I B T I M
F Q V T W W L B I Y Q D C P A J B
V E M F A P R N P X V U L B X P A
D I P M Q M S D E A J L E H I O K
P L A U N D R O M A T E C G T L E
G X H V C T U L N U T L T V A I R
W H T K G Q E I F E H W P G N C Y
S Z L S Y G K B D H E C P T L E Q
B P O V R E O R E M A E O R I L F
O X P N H O C A J B T X M A H S R
X I K K V T Z R T Q E I Y I S M J
T F H S M V C Y U E R T H N L C Z
Y F I R E D E P A R T M E N T J B
```

___ LIBRARY   ___ DEPARTMENT   ✔ LAUNDROMAT

___ THEATER   ___ SCHEDULE   ___ STATION

___ BUS   ___ VEHICLE   ✔ BAKERY

___ POLICE   ___ EXIT   ___ FIRE

___ TRAIN   ___ RESTAURANT   ___ TAXI

Job board.

Read the job ads. Write the missing information in the chart below.

Call 555-2402 Sea Siam Restaurant Cook Needed Part time $8.00/hr. Sat. and Sun. 9-6	Cobra Inc. Factory Worker Full time 8-5 Call 555-5111 $6.75	Spring Valley Library Custodian Needed Part time $4.75/hr. 3 evenings (M-W-F) 6-12 PM 555-8360	City Hall Secretary Full time M-F 8-5 $6.75 555-5600
Tip Top Nails Wanted! Manicurist Full time $5.25/hr. 8:00 AM to 6:00 PM (M-F) Call 555-4964	Duttonsville Bank Bank Teller M-F 9 AM - 1 PM $8.00 3 days a week Part time 555-6656	Nurse Needed! Royal Hospital 189 Orange Ave. Full time $18.75 12 AM - 8 AM Apply in person.	Joe's Garage Part time M &W 8-5 $9.75 Mechanic wanted Call 555-7040

JOB	HOURS	SALARY	FULL TIME YES	NO
bank teller	M-F 9am-1pm	$8.00 an hour		X
cook				
custodian				
factory worker				
manicurist				
mechanic				
nurse				
secretary				

Is she a teacher?

Is Sue Apple a teacher?	Is Sue Apple a barber?
Yes, she is.	No, she isn't.
She is a teacher.	She isn't a barber.

Answer the questions.

1. Pedro

   Is Pedro a mechanic?

   Yes, he is.

   He is a mechanic.

   _____

2. Juan

   Is Juan a secretary?

   No, he isn't.

   He isn't a secretary.

   He's a security guard.

3. Petra's mother

   Is Petra's mother a nurse?

   _____

   _____

   _____

Is he a gardener?

4. Hiroshi's father

Is Hiroshi's father a house painter?

_____

_____

5. Carlos

Is Carlos a gardener?

_____

_____

_____

6. Makeba

Is Makeba a nurse?

_____

_____

_____

7. Farima's sister

Is Farima's sister a nurse?

_____

_____

Who's working now? What's he/she doing?
Where's he/she working?

Nurse Needed!

Royal Hospital

189 Orange Ave.

Full time $18.75

12 AM - 8 AM

Cobra Inc.

Factory Worker

Full time 8-5

Call 555-5111 $6.75

Call 555-2402

Sea Siam Restaurant

Cook Needed

Part time $8.00/hr.

Sat. and Sun. 9-6

1. She is a nurse at Royal Hospital. She works full time. She earns $18.75 an hour.

2.

3.

Who's working now? What's he/she doing?
Where's he/she working?

City Hall

Secretary

Full time

M-F   8-5

$6.75

555-5600

Spring Valley Library

555-8360

Custodian Needed

Part time $7.75/hr.

3 evenings (M-W-F)

6-12 PM

Tip Top Nails

Wanted!

Manicurist

Full time $5.25/hr.

8:00 AM to 6:00 PM (M-F)

Call: 555-4964

4. _____

_____

_____

_____

_____

5. _____

_____

_____

_____

_____

6. _____

_____

_____

_____

_____

More about who's working.

A. Who's working now? What's she doing? Where's she working?

Duttonville School

Teacher Needed

English as a Second
Language

Part-time position

Monday to Friday

8 to 1

$20.00 per hour

_____

_____

_____

_____

_____

_____

B. What about you? Draw your own job ad. Write about you.

I _____

_____

_____

_____

_____

_____

UNIT 10 Crossword Puzzle

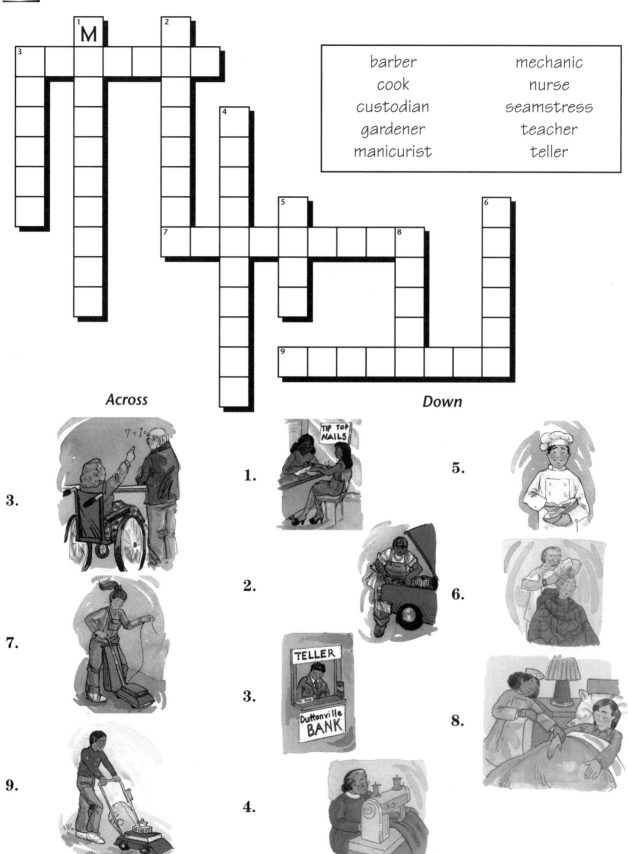

barber
cook
custodian
gardener
manicurist

mechanic
nurse
seamstress
teacher
teller

Across

3.

7.

9.

Down

1.

2.

3.

4.

5.

6.

8.

UNIT 10 Wordsearch

```
S E C R E T A R Y N Z N G R N V W D
T R L T Z H V E K S T O A Q V D R C
E Q R I E M A N I C U R I S T P L O
L O E U W F L Z J S M R N N J T N N
L T E A C H E R M E T B O E W I U S
E Z I W A X T E R J R U O J G R R T
R C U S T O D I A N C P A G A S S R
P V C D W G T L P N P S G S R W E U
D C H C O O K M F O R R U W D C C C
C Y J C Q U F V R B N P C O E U U T
X A Y K S Z J U Z H X Z S R N D R I
S A I T R A S S R T P E A K E K I O
B S J O F O F Q Q E Y B Y E R G T N
B F G X M E C H A N I C D R Y V Y D
A P F A C T O R Y D C X H J G P W S
N X N L M N B F P B L W Z Y J Y P A
K T F U P Q K O T A G U A R D L M X
S U T S L C G Y Y F G O N N B Y O M
```

___ **WORKER**   ___ **COOK**   ___ **BANK**

___ **CUSTODIAN**   ___ **SECRETARY**   ___ **FACTORY**

___ **TELLER**   ___ **MECHANIC**   ___ **MANICURIST**

___ **NURSE**   ___ **GARDENER**   ___ **TEACHER**

___ **SECURITY**   ✓ **GUARD**   ✓ **CONSTRUCTION**

UNIT 11

What's in the office?

A. Read the names of the office equipment.

1. telephone
2. computer keyboard
3. clothes-press machine

4. file cabinet
5. wastebasket
6. calculator

7. fax machine
8. typewriter
9. copier

B. Write the words under the pictures.

a.  He is using the ___fax machine___.	b.  She is using the _____.	c.  She is using the _____.
d.  He is using the _____.	e.  He is using the _____.	f.  He is using the _____.
g.  She is using the _____.	h.  She is using the _____.	i.  He is emptying the _____.

Can you read these signs?

Study the signs. Write the meanings under the pictures.

a. No! Stay out!
b. Shh-h-h!
c. You can't smoke here.

d. Emergency! Go out!
e. Men's restroom
f. This way to the telephone.

g. Be careful! Be cautious!
h. Danger. Don't touch.
i. Big trouble! Very dangerous.

j. Women's restroom
k. Don't go in there.
l. Go out this way every day.

DANGER

Big trouble!
Very dangerous.

EXIT

Women

Phone

Quiet!

Keep Out

Emergency Exit Only

CAUTION

Men

DO NOT ENTER

NO SMOKING

DO NOT TOUCH!

WATCH OUT, DON'T TOUCH!

Watch out, don't touch!
It's hot, you'll burn.
Let me show you how
to take your turn.

This machine is filled with heat.
You must be careful to retreat.
You might see the sign as you go
That reads, "Danger" or just "No!"

SIGNS OF THE TIMES

You can't smoke here!
This way to the phone.
Please be careful.
Sh-h-h-h. Quiet zone!

Women's room, men's room.
Exit now.
Danger and Caution.
Keep out and how!

Signs, signs everywhere.
Never did I know
Reading signs in English
Would help me go where I want to go.

What's it for? What's he/she doing?

a.

b.

c.

d.

e.

f.

g.

h.

i.

What are they doing? What are they using?
Write the letter of the picture.

_e_	**1.**	making copies		**6.**	emptying the wastebasket
___	**2.**	talking on the phone	___	**7.**	typing a letter
___	**3.**	using the calculator	___	**8.**	using the clothes-press machine
___	**4.**	using the computer	___	**9.**	filing papers
___	**5.**	sending a fax			

What are they doing in the office?

A. Write about the pictures.

1.

This is George.

He is working in the office.

He ___*is talking on the phone.*___

_____

2.

This is Grandpa.

He is working in the _____.

He _____

_____

3.

This is Theresa.

She is working _____.

She _____

_____

4.

This is Jack.

He is _____.

He _____

_____

5.

This is Dominique.

She _____ working in the _____.

She _____

_____

What are they doing in the office?

6.

This is Van.

He is working in the office.

He _____

_____

7.

This is Dominique.

She _____ in the office.

She _____

_____

8.

This is Jack

He is working in the factory.

He _____

_____

B. **What about you? Where are you? What are you doing now? Draw a picture of yourself at work or school.**

This is me.

I am studying/working at _____.

I _____

_____

_____

_____

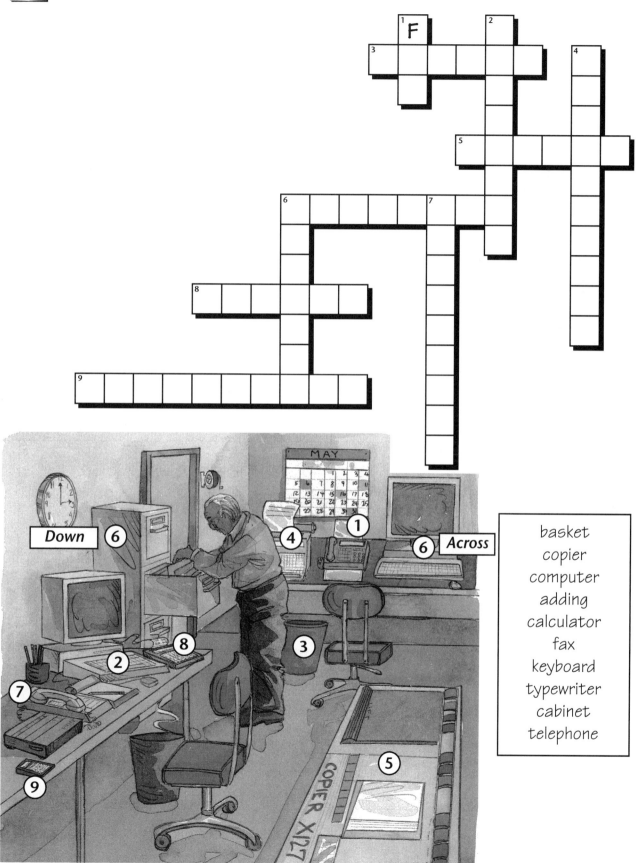

Down

Across

basket
copier
computer
adding
calculator
fax
keyboard
typewriter
cabinet
telephone

UNIT 11 Wordsearch

```
W  R  R  U  T  T  N  P  E  N  C  I  L  A  P  T  V  O
S  H  A  B  I  O  J  U  A  D  O  B  X  J  A  E  I  V
V  P  R  M  A  E  A  F  E  C  G  P  A  U  Q  D  B  Q
M  C  E  O  P  W  M  V  F  W  T  N  C  L  O  C  K  H
A  H  L  N  Z  R  I  U  H  G  P  S  J  Y  E  P  L  T
C  A  B  I  N  E  T  M  D  O  F  F  I  C  E  A  B  N
H  I  D  T  E  F  N  O  T  E  B  O  O  K  Q  B  I  C
I  R  M  O  Z  Q  T  E  L  E  P  H  O  N  E  L  S  A
N  Z  R  R  H  V  K  Z  F  F  A  X  J  Y  Q  C  W  Y
E  K  I  D  X  N  O  Y  K  W  O  U  R  G  R  E  H  X
T  Y  P  E  W  R  I  T  E  R  N  L  I  V  X  D  V  S
N  F  S  W  M  V  N  E  H  Q  M  P  A  D  I  A  G  H
S  T  C  L  Z  E  R  A  M  G  K  N  Y  F  R  I  D  W
C  A  L  C  U  L  A  T  O  R  B  B  O  J  C  L  Y  D
A  C  O  M  P  U  T  E  R  K  E  Y  B  O  A  R  D  E
P  N  J  W  P  I  J  W  T  H  S  Y  Z  P  V  B  S  S
P  M  V  E  K  L  B  S  C  R  E  E  N  M  S  H  N  K
K  U  A  E  T  D  T  W  Q  J  M  K  W  E  M  U  R  V
```

___ CABINET	___ MACHINE	✓ TYPEWRITER
___ COMPUTER	___ CLOCK	___ CALCULATOR
___ FAX	___ NOTEBOOK	___ TELEPHONE
___ PENCIL	___ KEYBOARD	___ CHAIR
___ OFFICE	✓ MONITOR	
___ SCREEN	___ DESK	

Do you want to live here?

What do you see?

	Yes	No
1. faucet dripping		✗
2. 3 bedrooms		
3. large yard		
4. leaking refrigerator		
5. cracked window		
6. broken door		
7. 2 bathrooms		
8. furniture		
9. washer and dryer		
10. toilet overflowing		
11. broken stove		
12. roof leaking		

Who fixes the problems?

the plumber   the repairman   the electrician   the TV repairman

Write a letter to the manager.

_____, _____

month   *date*   *year*

Dear Manager,

     I live in Apartment _____,

and the _____ is _____.

Would you please send the _____

as soon as possible to repair it?

         Thank you.

         Sincerely,

_____

_____, _____

month   *date*   *year*

Dear Manager,

     I live in Apartment _____,

and the _____ is _____.

Would you please send the _____

as soon as possible to repair it?

         Thank you.

         Sincerely,

_____

What's the problem?

What's the problem?	Fix it quick.
What's the problem?	Fix it quick.

TV's broken just won't click.

The roof is leaking.

The sink's a drip.

The heat is cold.

I'm in a snit.

What's the problem?	Fix it quick.
What's the problem?	Fix it quick.

The heat, the shower, the toilet, too.

Can't be fixed with spit and glue.

The window's cracked.

The stove is wrecked.

The lights are dark.

What am I to do?

What's the problem?	Fix it quick.
What's the problem?	Fix it quick.

Pick up the phone and give a call

to the manager down the hall.

Tell him or her to come quickly

The place's a mess, it's oh so icky.

All's not good. It's such a sight.

But, a manager's job is to set things right.

What's the problem?	Fix it quick.
What's the problem?	Fix it quick.

SPRING VALLEY NEWS
Classified Ads.

A. HOUSE FOR RENT	**B.** HOUSE	**C.** Clean Apartment
$950	321 Park Ave.	$725/mo.
2 bedrooms	$1,025/month	3 bedrooms
1 bathroom	3 bedrooms	2 bathrooms
	2 bathrooms	No pets
Near school	Furnished - washer, dryer, stove, and refrigerator	Near shopping
Call (715) 555-1434	OPEN HOUSE 9 to 5 daily	Call 555-3460
	555-8735	

D. House for Sale	**E.** FOR RENT	**F.** NEW HOUSE FOR SALE
NEW! CLEAN!	3 BDR. HOUSE/2 BA.	3 bedrooms
Near park/Near school	Unfurnished	2 bathrooms
3 bedrooms 2 baths	Near bus stop	Large yard
$150,000	Near shopping mall	Near library and school
Call (714) 555-4170	Call JONES REALTY	Open House: 8 to 5 daily
	555-9430	555-9321

G. Small Apartment		
$325 1 bedroom		
1 bath		
Quiet		
Call (714) 555-1004		

Can you find the ad?

1. What ad has an apartment for rent near shopping? _____C_____

2. What ad has a house for sale at $150,000? _____

3. What ad has a house for rent near a bus stop? _____

4. What ads show a house and an apartment with only one bathroom? _____

5. What ad shows a house for rent that is furnished? _____

6. What ad shows rent at $1,025? _____

7. What ad shows a house for sale near a school and a library? _____

Practice.

A. Draw a line.

1. open house
2. unfurnished
3. furnished
4. quiet
5. 9 to 5 daily
6. apt.
7. bdr.
8. ba.
9. no pets

a. bedroom
b. with furniture
c. bathroom
d. no dogs or cats, birds, etc.
e. apartment
f. open 9 A.M. to 5 P.M. every day
g. no furniture
h. go to visit the new house
i. quiet neighborhood

B. Make your own ad.

Spring Valley News

José is writing a letter to his wife.

three	tub	garage	two	stove
one	refrigerator	rent	shower	bedrooms

Help José write this letter to his wife. Read on page 141 and 142 about the house he rented. Look at the picture on page 143.

_____, _____
month   date   year

Dear Carlotta,

    I miss you and little Juanita very much. I am working very hard at two jobs, and I think of you and Juanita all the time.

    I have good news for you. Carlos and I found the perfect house for us to **1.** _____. This two-story house has **2.** _____ bedrooms. Two bedrooms are upstairs and **3.** _____ bedroom is downstairs. The house has **4.** _____ bathrooms. One bathroom is upstairs and the other is downstairs. Each bathroom has a **5.** _____ and a **6.** _____.

    The house is furnished and the kitchen has a **7.** _____ and a **8.** _____. In the **9.** _____, there is a washer and a dryer where we can wash and dry our clothes.

    The rent is perfect. I will pay a little more than Carlos because we will have the two **10.** _____ upstairs. One bedroom is for us, and the other is for Juanita.

    I love you and will write you more later. Kiss little Juanita for me.

                Your loving husband,
                José

UNIT 12 Crossword Puzzle

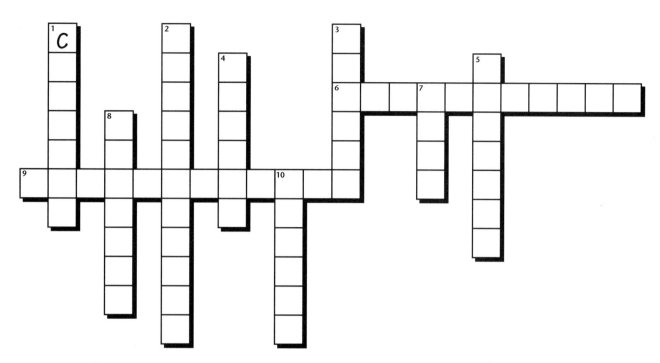

Across

6.

9.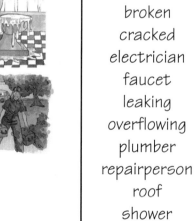

| broken |
| cracked |
| electrician |
| faucet |
| leaking |
| overflowing |
| plumber |
| repairperson |
| roof |
| shower |

Down

1.

2.

3.

4.

5.

7.

8.

10.

UNIT 12 Wordsearch

```
C U R J O G F A G F J N T R O T U
A I E B V N G C B F J Y Y Y X B T S
X A P A E A O W L V N O A R Q H V
M R A T R Q Z T X L K T R T J R U
D C I H F U R N I S H E D W P O G
O C R R L Q U E W F Q Z Q Q C O B
W G M O O I L L T O I L E T K F R
X I A O W V A E W E K H A X G J O
E F N M I I E C C S K B P H Y B K
E Y M L N R B T V R Y H A J O M E
G N E C G Z T R K R D L R Z N A N
L E A K I N G I H E S H T I R N F
I Z V H R L E C J Z J F M Q J A W
C J I E E P A I E P X E E M A G E
X P F E N B G A F Z I D N D X E N
H O V Q T T X N D C T U T C S R X
P L U M B E R W I N D O W K C M L
```

_____ **APARTMENT**   _____ **BROKEN**   _____ **BATHROOM**

_____ **ROOF**   _____ **YARD**   _____ **RENT**

_____ **LEAKING**   _____ **WINDOW**   ✓ **OVERFLOW**

_____ **REPAIRMAN**   _____ **MANAGER**   ✓ **PLUMBER**

_____ **FURNISHED**   _____ **ELECTRICIAN**   _____ **TOILET**

UNIT 13 It's a deal!

A. Read the story on page 145. Circle the correct answer.

1. José and Carlos ((like) / don't like) the house they saw.

2. They want to (buy / rent) the house.

3. They are (sad / happy).

4. They are also (excited / bored).

5. The price (is / isn't) right.

6. They say, ("It isn't a deal." / "It's a deal.").

7. It is a (good / bad) house for them.

B. Write a story. Copy the sentences.

José and Carlos like _____

_____

_____

_____

_____

_____

_____

_____

_____

_____

José and Carlos go to the bank.

A. **Read the words.**

a. ATM card **c.** credit card **e.** check **g.** ATM machine
b. checking account **d.** money order **f.** cash

B. **Write the words under the picture.**

1. _____

2. _____

3. _____

4. _____

5. __ATM card__

6. _____

7. _____

98

José and Carlos go to the post office.

Look at the picture and circle the best word. Write the sentence.

1.

José wants to mail this ((letter) / package).

José' wants _____

2.

Carlos needs to buy some (stamps / letters).

_____

3.

The (package / post card) is very heavy.

_____

4.

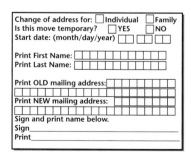

You can get a (Change of Address card / money order)
at the post office.

_____

I need to get some money orders.

A. Pay the phone bill: General Telephone.

$37.09

Bank of USA	DATE _March 3_ 19 _97_
MONEY ORDER	
PAY TO _General Telephone_	
AMOUNT _Thirty-seven dollars and ⁰⁹/₁₀₀_	$ _37.09_
Signature _José Arroyo_	Address _333 Pico Street, Duttonville_
003479:16790-0902	

B. Pay the water and trash bill: City of Duttonville.

$12.72

Bank of USA	DATE _____ 19 ____
MONEY ORDER	
PAY TO _____	
AMOUNT _____	$ _____
Signature _____	Address _____
003479:16790-0902	

C. Pay the electric bill: Edison Electric.

$20.24

Bank of USA	DATE _____ 19 ____
MONEY ORDER	
PAY TO _____	
AMOUNT _____	$ _____
Signature _____	Address _____
003479:16790-0902	

Let's mail our letters.

Address the envelope.

From:
Sue Apple
142 Pine Street
Spring Valley, CA 92234

To:
Edison Electric
1766 Olson Road
Spring Valley, CA 92238

> Sue Apple
> 142 Pine Street
> Spring Valley, CA 92234
>
> Edison Electric
> 1766 Olson Road
> Spring Valley, CA 92238

From:
José Arroyo
333 Pico Street
Duttonville, CA 92284

To:
Duttonville City Hall
16189 Grant Ave.
Duttonville, CA 92284

From:
YOU
Your address

To:
YOUR SCHOOL
Ask your teacher for
the address.

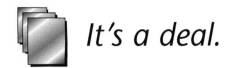

It's a deal.

IT'S A DEAL

It's a deal.
It's such a deal.
How, in fact,
Can it be real?

Two for one
and
Four for two.
Do I need to buy
this extra shoe?

It's a deal.
It's such a deal.
How, in fact,
Can it be real?

This is half off
and
that is, too.
I'll take two more
Both in blue.

It's a deal.
It's such a deal.
How, in fact,
Can it be real?

This rent is cheap.
The price is right.
I'll take that house.
This is out of sight.

It's a deal.
It's such a deal.
How, in fact,
Can it be real?

Let's shake hands
that we agree.
We're so happy,
Let's drink tea.

It's a deal.
It's such a deal.
How, in fact,
Can it be real?

UNIT 13 Crossword Puzzle

Across

2. What the post office delivers

M _ _ _

4. Place for money

B _ _ _

6. What you mail at the post office

P _ _ _ _ _ _

8. You don't always buy a house, you can

R _ _ _

9. What you write to pay your bills

C _ _ _ _

Down

1. What you place on an envelope

S _ _ _ _

3. What the post office delivers

L _ _ _ _ _ _

5. You go to the ATM for

C _ _ _

7. Where you live

A _ _ _ _ _ _

UNIT 13 Wordsearch

```
C X N D B Y J R Y E B H I B X G Z
U B C T Z C U Z I O A Z I D H X B
S D R C L D W A J J N Q X J L R B
N C E A J E G F N E K S V U N B
X P D S O A M Q E B I L G C N F C
V L I H R L M R P Y M E M E B Z A
W U T M Y B V V A R O T M C C P R
Y P Z A T C P F C P Y T H M J R D
N A P I F H W M K B H E C O R H C
D Y P L Y A W X A V M R H N J M J
W W B U U N N P G T Q Z E E J Y P
G D S A L G K I E P N Y C Y Y A F
B I T T X E P P Z J U G K X W F J
H T A M Y S E A M O U N T B Y V R
L T M U Y J Q K G K E D S D H B H
O A P A Z T D G W P B U K Y K S H
X Z D O B A D D R E S S P B G M C
```

___ **BANK**   ___ **CASH**   ___ **CREDIT**   ___ **ATM**

___ **STAMP**   ___ **LETTER**   ___ **PACKAGE**   ___ **MONEY**

✓ **AMOUNT**   ___ **CHECK**   ✓ **MAIL**   ___ **PAY**

___ **CHANGE**   ___ **ADDRESS**   ___ **DEAL**   ___ **CARD**

Bic, you're lazy at home.

A. Read the conversation on page 157. Circle the correct answer.

1. (Charlie / (Rose)) is upset with Bic.

2. Bic is (hard-working / lazy) at home.

3. He (looks / doesn't look) clean.

4. Bic's room (is / isn't) messy.

5. Bic (comes / doesn't come) home early.

6. He (drives / walks) too fast.

7. He (smokes / doesn't smoke) too much.

B. Write the story.

Rose is upset with Bic.

_____

_____

_____

_____

_____

_____

_____

Are you angry?   Are you pleased?

1. angry
2. fast
3. messy
4. quiet

5. clean
6. hard-working
7. neat
8. slow

9. dirty
10. late
11. noisy
12. too little

13. early
14. lazy
15. pleased
16. too much

A. **Find the correct word. Complete the sentence.**

1. Jose wasn't angry.   He was __*pleased*__ .

2. Carlos isn't messy.   He is _____ .

3. Petra is early.   She isn't _____ .

4. Bic isn't hard-working.   He is _____ .

5. Grandpa isn't noisy.   He is _____ .

6. Your desk isn't dirty.   It is _____ .

7. Bic's car isn't slow.   It is _____ .

B. **What about you? Circle the best answer.**

1. I'm (messy / neat).

2. I like to be (late / early).

3. I am usually (lazy / hard-working)

4. I like (quiet / noisy) people.

C. **Write about you.**

_____

_____

_____

_____

_____

What do your classmates like?
What don't they like?

A. Find someone who. . .

Name	
	likes fast cars. (Do you like fast cars?)
	doesn't like fast cars.
	is quiet. (Are you quiet?)
	is sometimes noisy.
	likes talking on the phone. (Do you like to talk . . .)
	doesn't like talking on the phone.
	likes a lot of makeup. (Do you like a lot of . . .)
	doesn't like makeup.

B. What about you? Circle *Yes* or *No.*

Yes	**No**	I like fast cars.
Yes	**No**	I don't like fast cars.
Yes	**No**	I am quiet.
Yes	**No**	I am sometimes noisy.
Yes	**No**	I like talking on the phone.
Yes	**No**	I don't like talking on the phone.
Yes	**No**	I like a lot of makeup.
Yes	**No**	I don't like makeup.

This or that?

THIS OR THAT?

Are you angry?

Are you lazy?

Are you early?

Are you pleased?

Do you work with ease?

Are you late?

Do you have a lot of trouble keeping that date?

Do you have too little?

Do you like being dirty?

Do you have too much?

Do you clean and such?

Are you quiet all day?

Are you neat as a pin?

Do you drive too fast?

Make noise at night?

Does your mess cause a fright?

Do you drive too slow?

Or do you take the bus to go where you go?

Whatever we are

We know for a fact

We're either this

Or we're either that.

TAKING THE MESSAGE

Can I take a message?

Can I tell him of your call?

Shall I tell him that you'll meet him

At three at the mall?

I'm writing down your number

Please tell me that again.

I hope that I can remember

To take all your message in.

I promise you I'll leave a note.

Here beside the phone.

When my roommate gets it,

You'll hear the happy tone.

What do you look like?

A. Draw your face.
Add these labels.

eye	eyelash
eyebrow	ear
cheek	lips
teeth	neck

B. Draw what you are wearing.
Add these labels.

shirt—blouse—T–shirt

skirt—pants—dress

shorts—tennis shoes

sandals—shoes—socks

C. Describe yourself.
Ask your teacher for help.

I am (short / tall).

I have _____ eyes.
        color

I have _____ hair.
        color

I have (long / short) hair.

I have (straight / curly / wavy) hair.

D. Write something special about yourself.

_____

_____

_____

What do your classmates look like?

Ask your classmates these questions. Write their names.

Are you. . . ?

Do you have. . . ?

tall

black/brown hair

blond hair

short

short hair

long hair

straight hair

curly hair

Across

2.

5.

6.

7.

9.

| angry |
| clean |
| dirty |
| early |
| hard-working |
| late |
| lazy |
| messy |
| neat |

Down

1.

3.

4.

8.

UNIT 14 Wordsearch

```
Q  H  P  K  D  D  A  E  B  N  N  E  R  U  V  L  G
G  A  T  Y  E  A  L  H  E  A  V  Y  O  B  C  E  D
F  A  S  T  K  N  Y  Q  P  A  L  N  X  X  M  Y  L
O  L  E  K  S  G  K  S  G  T  Y  E  F  X  A  E  O
B  H  Y  X  O  R  A  B  Y  C  B  C  F  X  G  L  J
F  O  E  T  B  Y  Q  M  D  U  J  K  F  Y  K  A  F
T  J  B  E  M  G  O  V  K  R  K  Q  V  B  D  S  K
O  L  R  E  C  U  H  R  J  L  T  F  A  R  P  H  C
S  R  O  T  I  I  P  S  U  Y  J  M  V  A  R  S  H
T  C  W  H  C  R  V  C  K  V  C  W  E  Y  U  T  X
C  E  O  B  E  W  F  F  A  C  E  Z  E  X  E  R  W
S  L  O  W  K  L  Q  J  M  X  R  D  F  Y  G  A  Z
U  X  S  P  K  Z  U  X  C  B  J  I  D  V  V  I  G
P  F  S  K  M  E  S  S  Y  Q  D  R  A  V  B  G  Q
R  O  S  I  T  G  D  B  D  S  H  T  A  S  T  H  K
L  V  D  T  L  Z  N  E  A  R  L  Y  Y  G  O  T  V
L  A  Z  Y  N  O  I  S  Y  T  Q  U  I  E  T  I  S
```

___ EYEBROW	___ EYELASH	✔ CURLY	___ NOISY
___ NECK	___ STRAIGHT	___ QUIET	___ FAST
___ HEAVY	___ ANGRY	✔ EARLY	
___ LAZY	___ MESSY	___ FACE	
___ SLOW	___ TEETH	___ DIRTY	

Complete.

celebration   **end of the school term**   **housewarming**   **potluck**

1. A "_____" is a party where every one brings food.

2. A "_____" is a celebration for a new home. Everyone usually brings a small gift for the house.

3. The "_____" is the time when classes are over. We say "good-bye" to our class and teacher.

4. A "_____" is having a good time at a potluck, housewarming, or end of the school term.

What's your favorite celebration?

A. **Write about your favorite celebration in your country.**

My name is _____, and I am from

_____. In my country,

_____ is my favorite celebration.

This celebration is held on _____ _____ this year.
                                            month   *date*

On this special day, I like to _____

_____

_____.

B. **Now draw a picture of your favorite celebration.**

Food for a party!

A. Read the words.

1. chips
2. egg rolls
3. pizza

4. juice
5. sushi
6. salad

7. tortillas
8. pita bread
9. meat and rice

10. salsa
11. hot dogs
12. sandwiches

B. Complete the sentences.

Pedro

1. Pedro likes _____ and

_____, but he doesn't like

_____.

Farima

2. Farima likes _____ and

_____, but she doesn't like

_____.

Van Ly

3. Van Ly likes _____ and

_____, but he doesn't like

_____.

Makeba

4. Makeba likes _____ and

_____, but she doesn't like

_____.

Food for a party!

Hiroshi   **Sue**

5. Hiroshi likes _____ and **6.** Sue likes _____ and

_____, but he doesn't like   _____, but she doesn't like

_____.   _____.

C. **What about you?** Draw the kinds of food you like, and write about them.

_____	_____	_____

_____	_____	_____

I like _____, _____,

_____, and _____, but I don't like

_____.

What I like, and what we both like.

1. bananas
2. beans
3. beef
4. chips
5. egg rolls
6. bread
7. broccoli
8. butter

9. cabbages
10. cakes
11. pizza
12. sushi
13. carrots
14. salad
15. chicken
16. tortillas

17. coffee
18. meat/rice
19. cookies
20. fish
21. pita bread
22. ice cream
23. salsa
24. hot dogs

25. sandwiches
26. peaches
27. rice
28. tea
29. sodas
30. pork
31. potatoes
32. pasta

Work with a partner to fill in the boxes with the words above or your own favorite foods.

I like	We like	_____ likes

The end of the school term is here.

A. **Write about your school term.**

Today is _____ _____, _____.
                    month   *date*   *year*

I want to remember my teacher, my new classmates, and friends.

My school is _____ in the city of

_____ in the state of _____.

I studied in Room _____, and my teacher's name is _____.

My new friends are _____ , _____,

_____, _____ and

_____. I will miss everyone.

B. **Design a goodbye card. Cut it out and give to your best friend.**

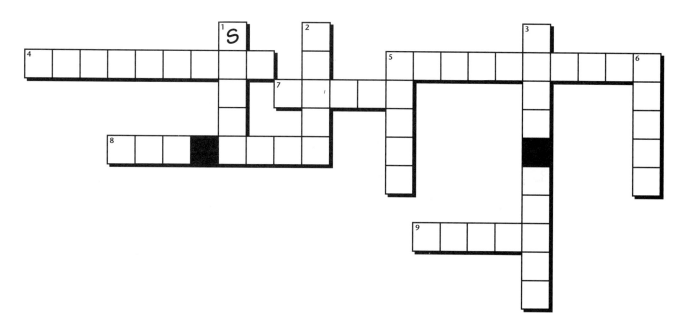

Across

4.

5.

7.

8.

9.

chips
hot dogs
juice
pita bread
pizza
salad
salsa
sandwiches
sushi
tortillas

Down

1.

2.

3.

5.

6.

UNIT 15 *Wordsearch*

```
O  B  E  V  Z  H  J  E  S  A  L  S  A  H  B  R  D
K  Y  A  S  U  S  H  I  A  V  D  P  H  B  J  B  H
V  I  S  S  U  X  O  C  O  L  U  M  B  U  S  C  I
T  N  T  A  U  S  A  N  D  W  I  C  H  E  S  T  B
V  D  E  L  S  H  R  J  Q  R  N  I  W  U  J  H  W
A  E  R  A  C  E  L  E  B  R  A  T  I  O  N  A  M
Z  P  V  D  T  K  V  R  E  S  C  M  V  K  N  N  F
O  E  T  R  C  P  P  O  T  L  U  C  K  T  G  K  U
B  N  Y  V  H  A  V  A  L  E  N  T  I  N  E  S  Z
R  D  N  P  R  R  C  P  L  A  N  R  P  K  U  G  G
A  E  P  P  I  T  B  I  O  K  Q  O  K  C  S  I  E
M  N  I  H  S  Y  E  M  E  M  O  R  I  A  L  V  M
A  C  Z  L  T  O  R  T  I  L  L  A  S  T  P  I  W
D  E  Z  V  M  C  H  I  P  S  E  X  X  J  N  N  C
A  V  A  P  A  S  V  M  I  G  Y  H  L  P  Z  G  N
N  G  O  J  S  N  P  C  T  K  Q  X  B  U  C  F  I
L  Q  S  J  J  D  H  A  L  L  O  W  E  E  N  L  X
```

___ **PARTY**

___ **MEMORIAL**

___ **RAMADAN**

___ **HALLOWEEN**

___ **PIZZA**

___ **SUSHI**

___ **SANDWICHES**

___ **CELEBRATION**

___ **THANKSGIVING**

___ **VALENTINES**

✓ **COLUMBUS**

___ **CHIPS**

✓ **SALAD**

___ **POTLUCK**

___ **CHRISTMAS**

___ **EASTER**

___ **INDEPENDENCE**

___ **SALSA**

___ **TORTILLA**